Stories
of
Wizards

Stories
of
Wizards

Gillian Doherty

Illustrated by Linda Edwards

Designed by Amanda Gulliver, Mary Cartwright
and Michelle Lawrence

Edited by Anna Milbourne

Contents

The sorcerer's apprentice

When Hans became the sorcerer's apprentice, it seemed like a dream come true. But the reality turned out to be rather different. All he ever got to do was dust magic books, clean out cauldrons and weed the enchanted herb garden.

"This is boring," Hans complained to his master. "When do I get to learn some magic? I want to conjure up a castle with a moat filled with sharks and have my very own pet dragon."

"This isn't a game," said the sorcerer sternly. "You will learn when the time is right." Hans fidgeted and looked down at his feet. He didn't like being told off.

The next morning, the sorcerer called Hans into his study. "I've got to go out now," he said, "and I'm leaving you in charge."

The boy's face lit up. This was just the opportunity he had been waiting for.

"While I'm away," continued the sorcerer, "I want you to scrub the castle floors until they sparkle. I'll inspect them when I get back, so make sure you do a good job."

Hans groaned. The floors were black with years of grime and soot. He couldn't imagine them ever being clean again.

"It's not fair," he grumbled when his master had gone. "He treats me like a servant. Why should I spend all afternoon on my hands and knees when with a wave of his wand he could have it all done in an instant?"

Suddenly, Hans had an idea. "What's to stop me from giving it a try?" he thought. The sorcerer's wand was lying there on the desk. He picked it up and waved it in the air. Nothing happened.

He closed his eyes. "I wish the castle was clean," he whispered and waved the wand again. But when he opened his eyes, everything looked exactly the same as before.

Hans looked around thoughtfully. He caught sight of the sorcerer's spell book right on top of the bookcase. "That's what I need!" he exclaimed. He dragged a chair over and clambered onto it.

The book was still too high for him to reach, so he climbed up the shelves, using them like a ladder.

When he got to the top, Hans reached up and took down the book. It was very heavy indeed. He tucked it under his arm and climbed carefully down, clinging to the shelves with his free hand.

As Hans opened the spell book, he felt the most incredible thrill. It was as though all the world's wisdom lay before him. There were spells to turn frogs into princes, princes to stone and just about everything to gold. The pages of the book were yellow with age and terribly fragile. He turned them carefully, hardly daring to breathe in case they crumbled to dust.

Eventually, Hans found what he was looking for: "How to bring a broomstick to life". He picked up the wand and pointed it at the broomstick in the corner. Then he read the spell aloud: "Little broomstick, do as I ask. Stand to attention and await your task."

At once, two arms sprouted from the handle and the knots in the wood became two wrinkly eyes. The broomstick jumped up and gave a neat salute. Hans could hardly believe it. The spell had worked.

"Well, what are you waiting for?" he said. "Fetch some water and clean this castle."

The next thing he knew, the broomstick was racing out of the door with a bucket in each hand.

Just a few seconds later it was back again, sloshing water all over the floor. It scurried around, scrubbing under the table, behind all the chairs and in every last nook and cranny. Then it grabbed the empty buckets and dashed outside.

"Just wait until the sorcerer sees this," chuckled Hans. "He'll be so impressed."

But the busy broomstick hadn't finished yet. It bounded back into the room with two buckets full of water and started to wash down the walls.

Feeling rather smug, Hans settled himself down in the sorcerer's rocking chair to watch. "This is more like it," he said to himself. As he rocked back and forth, his head began to nod and before long he was fast asleep.

Hans dreamed that he was sailing on the wide, blue ocean. The waves rocked the boat gently from side to side and seagulls soared overhead, gliding on the breeze. Then a huge wave rose up out of nowhere. It crashed over the side of the boat, almost sweeping him away.

Hans woke up with a jolt, gasping and spluttering for air. The broomstick was standing over him with a bucket in each hand and he was drenched from head to toe. "What's going on?" cried Hans. "You're not supposed to be cleaning *me*."

The broomstick stared blankly at him. Then it turned to go. Hans tried to stand up, but the rocking chair was no longer standing on the ground; it was floating. "What have you done?" he wailed.

The broomstick didn't answer. It just splashed right out of the door. Hans waded after it. "That's enough," he said. "I'm your master and you must do as you're told."

But when the broomstick returned, it was carrying even more water. Hans started to panic. "Clean up this mess," he said in as firm a voice as he could manage.

The broomstick didn't do anything of the sort. It simply emptied the buckets and raced outside.

Hans ran over to the spell book and began to search frantically through the pages. There were thousands of spells to do all kinds of things, but he couldn't find anything at all that would stop the broomstick.

He tried to think of any words he knew that sounded even remotely magical. "Abracadabra, alakazam, algebra..." he began. "Hey presto, heebie-jeebies, higgledy piggledy, hocus pocus, hullaballoo...mumbo jumbo, open sesame, zip-a-dee-doo-dah."

None of them had the slightest effect. Hans tried to grab hold of the broomstick, but it sidestepped nimbly and he fell face down in the water. He stood up, dripping wet and very angry indeed. "Stop right now," he spluttered. "If you don't, I'll..."

Hans stopped in mid-sentence. What could he do? He had no power over the broomstick and no idea whatsoever how to make it stop.

Then he spotted a hatchet by the fireplace. The situation called for drastic measures. He picked it up and hid behind the open door.

As soon as the broomstick burst in again, he leaped out and brought down the blade. Crack! It split the broomstick right in two.

"Thank goodness it's over," sighed Hans, wiping his brow. Then, to his absolute horror, little green shoots popped out of the broken pieces. Hans watched in utter dismay as they grew into arms. "This c-c-can't be happening," he stammered.

But it was. A moment later, not one, but two broomsticks were standing before him. They blinked, and then turned and ran outside to fetch more water.

Now the water was flooding in twice as fast as before. Hans watched helplessly as it rose higher and higher.

12

"My master's going to kill me," he thought. He started to scoop the water out of the door with his hands, but there was far too much of it and more was flooding in all the time.

Hans chased after one of the broomsticks and tried to catch hold of it, but the other one beat him back. He ran after the other one and the same thing happened.

Eventually, he saw red. "I'll show you who's the boss around here," he yelled, and swung the hatchet at them wildly. Pieces of wood flew everywhere, but Hans didn't stop; he whirled around in a chopping frenzy until all that was left of the broomsticks were tiny splinters floating on the water.

"I'd better get things back in order before the sorcerer comes back," he panted. He filled a bucket with water and threw it out of the door.

When he turned back to scoop up another, his mouth dropped open. The splinters were growing. One after the other, they sprang to their feet, and soon there was a whole army of broomsticks lined up in rows before him. They stood to attention and then began to march, left-right, left-right, towards the door.

Suddenly, they came to an abrupt halt. Standing in the doorway with his arms folded and a formidable look on his face was the sorcerer.

Hans felt a strange mixture of fear and relief. "I'm so sorry," he whimpered. "I was just trying to clean the castle. I didn't mean to cause any trouble."

The sorcerer frowned at him. Then he raised his arms and chanted:

"Stop now, broomsticks.

Enough is enough.

Obey your master and stop this fuss."

Immediately, the broomsticks stood to attention, awaiting their orders. "Clean up this mess at once," commanded the sorcerer.

There was a burst of activity as the broomsticks rushed around, chasing the water out of the door and back down to the river.

"Good," said the sorcerer when they had finished. "Now, I only need one broomstick. The rest of you be gone." He waved his wand and the army of broomsticks vanished. Just his own broomstick was left. "Back to your place," he ordered it.

The broomstick trotted obediently over to the corner, leaned itself against the wall and became an ordinary broomstick once more.

Hans let out an enormous sigh. He had never been so relieved in all his life.

With calm restored at last, the sorcerer turned to him. "A little knowledge is a dangerous thing," he said quietly. "It takes years to learn how to control magic."

"Don't worry," said Hans. "I've learned my lesson. It will be a long time before I try my hand at magic again."

Ivan and the firebird

Prince Ivan was riding in the forest one crisp winter's day when he saw a flash of red and gold in the trees ahead. It looked as if the branches themselves were ablaze. When he got closer, he found that it was not a fire, but an extraordinary bird, with feathers that shimmered like dancing flames as it flitted between the trees.

Enchanted by the firebird's beauty, Ivan set off in pursuit. It drew him deeper and deeper into the forest, always staying just out of reach.

For seven days and seven nights Ivan chased after it. He was totally exhausted. When, at last, the firebird settled on the lower branch of a tree, he saw his chance. Sliding down from his horse, he crept up behind the bird and made a grab for it.

The firebird struggled to escape, but Ivan held on. Then, to his amazement, the creature spoke. "Please release me," it said. Its light was starting to fade and Ivan realized it would be cruel to keep it.

Reluctantly, he let the bird go and it flew up into a tree. "You won't be sorry," said the firebird, its glow already returning. It plucked out one of its feathers and let it drift down on the breeze. "Keep this feather safe," it said. "If ever you're in trouble, just hold it in the air and I will come."

"Thank you..." Ivan began, but the firebird had already disappeared. Suddenly, he realized he was lost. He had been so absorbed by the chase that he hadn't noticed where the firebird was leading him and now he was all alone.

Ivan looked around to see where it had gone. To his relief, he saw something shining in the distance. "Wait!" he shouted. He leaped onto his horse and galloped through the trees towards it.

Instead of the firebird, he found a magnificent palace topped with golden domes. It was surrounded by a wall, but one of the gates was open, so he slipped into the garden.

There was something unnatural about this garden. In the middle stood a tree bearing golden apples and all around were statues of knights and their horses. They weren't at all the sort of statues you would expect to find in a palace garden. They were frozen in all kinds of strange poses and their faces were contorted as if they were in pain.

Just then, one of the palace doors
opened. Quickly, Ivan hid behind a tree.
    Twelve pretty princesses ran outside.
"Come on, Vasilisa," called the last one.
She looked back and held out her hand.
    The thirteenth princess stepped
outside. She was the most beautiful
of all and yet she had the saddest
face Ivan had ever seen. She shook
her head.
    "Suit yourself," said the girl
and ran to join the others.

The twelve princesses began to dance together by the light of the moon, but Vasilisa sat down a little way away from them. She looked so lonely that Ivan couldn't bear it. He came out from his hiding place and took a step towards her.

When the princesses saw him, they shrank together in fear. "Who are you?" asked Vasilisa.

"My name is Ivan," said the prince. "Please don't be afraid. I lost my way in the forest and came across this palace."

"Well, you'll wish you never had," said Vasilisa mournfully. She gestured at the statues. "This is what happens to visitors here. We are all the prisoners of Koschei the deathless."

Ivan felt a shiver run down his spine. He had heard of the wizard Koschei, but hardly believed that he really existed. "Couldn't you escape?" he asked. "This gate is open. There's nothing to stop you."

"If only it were so easy," sighed Vasilisa. "It is magic that keeps us here. We can only come into this garden by night, and if any of us tries to leave we will all die. You are free though. You must go while you still can."

"I can't just leave you here," said Prince Ivan. "There must be some way to break the magic."

"It's impossible," she said. "Koschei is too powerful. The magic will last for as long as he lives, and he has already lived longer than anyone can remember. He keeps his soul hidden away. While it is safe, he will never die."

In spite of Vasilisa's warnings, Ivan was determined to try.

Too soon, the rosy rays of dawn began to creep across the sky. "Our time is up," said Vasilisa. "We must go." The thirteen princesses ran towards the palace.

When she got to the door, Vasilisa stopped and looked back. "Be careful," she called. Then she darted inside and the door slammed shut behind her.

Ivan banged on the door with his fist. "What do you want?" said a hollow voice behind him.

He turned to find Koschei towering over him. The wizard had a wild, flame-red beard and angry eyebrows. "I demand that you set the princesses free," said Ivan bravely.

"How dare you!" thundered Koschei. "You're in no position to make demands." He pointed at Ivan and began to mutter a spell.

All kinds of strange monsters appeared.
Some had scaly bodies and spikes along their
backs. Others had leathery wings or horns.
They surrounded the prince, baring their
teeth and snatching at him with their claws.
No matter how brave he was, Prince Ivan
was no match for all of them.

Then Ivan remembered what
the firebird had said to him. He took
out the feather and held it high
above his head.

There was a whooshing
sound and the firebird swept
into the garden. It had come,
just as it said it would.

These ugly creatures had never seen anything so beautiful. They staggered towards the firebird, falling all over one another in their desire to capture it, but it whirled around them in a blur of red and gold.

When the monsters were so dizzy they could barely stand, the firebird landed in the apple tree and began to sing. Ivan's heart ached as he listened to it.

The melody soared effortlessly on the breeze, captivating the monsters too. They swayed in time with the music. Gradually, their eyes began to droop and the strange lullaby carried them into a magical sleep.

During all this time, Koschei was silent, but he had a glazed look in his eyes and he wasn't moving. It seemed that even the great wizard was not beyond the firebird's charms.

"Quickly, there isn't much time," said the firebird. "My magic has taken Koschei by surprise, but it won't last for long. Buried beneath this tree is a chest which contains an egg. Koschei keeps his soul inside that egg. Destroy it and you will bring his evil magic to an end."

Ivan didn't waste any time. Kneeling down, he began to dig with his bare hands. It was hard work, but he kept going and after a few minutes his fingers touched something hard. He scraped away the earth to reveal a brightly painted chest. Eagerly, Ivan heaved the chest out of the hole. It was locked. He picked up a large stone and pounded the lock until it smashed. Then he flung open the lid. Lying inside the chest was a shining golden egg.

As Ivan reached out to pick up the egg, the firebird let out a cry. Koschei had awoken from his trance. When he saw what Ivan was doing, he flew at him, his face twisted with rage.

"Stay where you are," warned Ivan, seizing the egg.

Koschei stopped in his tracks. "You don't know what you're doing," he snarled. "Give that to me."

Ivan shook his head. "First, you must set your prisoners free," he said.

Koschei growled and took a step closer.

"Keep back or I'll drop it," threatened Ivan.

Unable to hold back any longer, Koschei made a grab for the egg.

Ivan let go. With a blood-curdling scream, the wizard dived to catch it, but before he could get there the egg hit the ground and smashed into tiny pieces.

The wizard thudded down after it, his hand clutching at the air in a final moment of desperation. Ivan saw the life drain from his eyes. Koschei the deathless was dead.

Immediately, his magic began to slip away. The golden apples fell to the ground and withered, and the tangled vines of the forest crept over the wall. Everything was returning to how it had been before.

The stone figures came back to life too. The knights blinked in bewilderment, scarcely able to believe they were living and breathing again, and their horses shook their manes and stamped their feet.

Finally, the palace itself began to crumble. Ivan flung open the door and the thirteen princesses rushed outside.

"Quickly!" he cried. "It's collapsing." He took Vasilisa's hand and they all ran for their lives. Behind them, there was a deafening crash as the palace walls tumbled to the ground.

Only when they were well out of harm's way did they stop running and look back. Where the palace had been, there was just a heap of dust.

Vasilisa turned to Ivan. "Can it be true?" she said. "Have you done the impossible?"

"It's true," said Ivan. "Nothing is impossible. With the firebird's help, I have defeated Koschei, and now it's time to go home." He helped Vasilisa onto his horse and climbed on behind her.

"Come with us," he called to the others. "Koschei is dead. You're free to go."

Eager to get away, the knights and princesses got on the horses and galloped after them.

The firebird flew ahead, guiding the way with its magical light. For seven days and seven nights, they followed it through the forest.

At last, they reached Prince Ivan's castle. "This is where I must leave you," said the firebird. "Your future awaits." Then, blazing like the rising sun, it soared up into the sky.

The stolen bride

Ruslan and Ludmilla could not have been happier. It was their wedding day and all their friends and family had gathered at the palace. Everyone was laughing and chattering when suddenly the door burst open.

Before they knew what was happening, the terrified guests were swept aside. A tornado blasted right through the hall and swirled around Ludmilla. She felt invisible hands take hold of her and found herself being lifted off the ground. Ruslan tried to pull her back, but the hands pushed him away.

Ludmilla was carried away from the palace and up into the air. She struggled and fought, trying desperately to escape, but it was no use. She went higher and higher, and became so breathless and dizzy that she fainted.

When Ludmilla came to her senses, she was lying on a huge oak bed, surrounded by silk curtains. She could hear a harp playing, although there was no musician anywhere to be seen. "Where am I?" she murmured.

Then she remembered what had happened. She rushed to the door and found it locked. In a panic, she ran over to the window. It was open, but much too high to climb out of. Below there were pretty gardens, beyond which lay a carpet of forest that extended as far as she could see.

It was no use calling for help. There was no one for miles around to hear her. Ludmilla threw herself on the bed and began to sob.

After a while, there was a knock at the door and a servant entered. "The wizard Chernomor," he announced with a flourish. But, instead of a wizard, a line of servants marched in, each carrying a plump velvet cushion. Draped ceremoniously across the cushions was a long, silvery beard, at the end of which was its unlikely owner – an eccentric-looking hunchbacked dwarf.

"You're a wizard?" said Ludmilla, barely able to conceal her astonishment.

"I am indeed," replied Chernomor pompously. "I trust everything is to your satisfaction."

She stifled a giggle. It was hard to be afraid of such a ridiculous creature.

The dwarf frowned. If there was one thing he hated more than anything else it was being laughed at. He took what he imagined was a menacing step towards her, but somehow he got caught up in his own beard and fell head over heels. He tried to get to his feet, but he was so tangled up that he fell over again and again, and in the end his servants had to carry him away to be unwound.

When they had gone, Ludmilla noticed the dwarf's hat lying on the floor. She put it on and looked in the mirror. The hat looked almost as comical on her as it did on him. Amused, she tipped it forward and back, and tilted it to one side, making funny faces at herself in the mirror. Then she turned the hat around so that it was facing backwards. At this, Ludmilla let out a gasp. Her reflection had disappeared. She turned the hat back and there she was.

Ludmilla heard footsteps in the corridor. Quickly, she turned the hat backwards again. She was just in time. A split second after she disappeared, the door burst open. Chernomor stopped dead. "Where's the girl?" he demanded.

His servants looked under the bed, behind the curtains and in all the cupboards. They couldn't find Ludmilla anywhere, which was hardly surprising since she had already sneaked past them and was hurrying down the stairs.

As soon as she was outside, Ludmilla ran as fast as she could to the gate. To her dismay, it was locked. There was no escape. "Ruslan!" she called in desperation. "Where are you? Please help me."

Chernomor heard her cry and looked out of the window. He could see the gate being shaken, but he couldn't see Ludmilla. Then a thought struck him. He reached up and patted his head. Sure enough, his hat was missing. "Just as I thought," he growled. "She's stolen my invisibility hat."

He ordered his servants to search the gardens. They hunted from morning until night, but try as they might they couldn't find her. As long as Ludmilla kept quiet, it was easy for her to avoid them.

The days passed by and Chernomor grew more and more frustrated. Every now and then, he would see signs of her — an apple floating down from a tree, an invisible hand breaking the water of the fountain, or a sorrowful song carried on the breeze — but by the time he got there, she was always gone.

At last, Chernomor had an idea. "I know just the way to catch her," he thought. He stroked his beard once, twice, three times, and then magically he began to change until he looked exactly like Ruslan. He looked at his reflection in the mirror. "Goodness knows what she sees in him," he sneered.

With this cunning disguise, Chernomor went out into the garden. "Ludmilla," he called. "Come here, my darling."

When Ludmilla heard his voice, her heart leaped with joy. It sounded exactly like Ruslan. She ran through the garden and into his arms. "I knew you would come," she cried happily. Yet, as his embrace closed around her, she knew that something was wrong. She tried to pull away, but his grip tightened.

Then he began to change. His nose grew longer, hair sprouted from his chin and he started to shrink. Soon, Chernomor was no higher than Ludmilla's waist. He reached up and knocked the hat off her head. "You won't escape again," he snarled as she reappeared. "I'm going to make you my wife before the day is out."

"I'll never marry you," cried Ludmilla. "You're not half the man Ruslan is. He'll rescue me. I know he will."

"We'll see about that," said Chernomor. He dragged Ludmilla back to her room and locked the door.

Ludmilla paced up and down for hours, trying to think of a way to escape. Eventually, she lay down and fell into an exhausted sleep. She dreamed that three maids came to her room. Silently, they brushed her hair, dressed her in a bridal gown and placed a crown of pearls on her head. She tried to resist, but she couldn't.

Suddenly, she woke up in a feverish state. Chernomor was standing in the doorway, looking even more ludicrous than usual. His beard was decorated with bright pink bows, his velvet cloak was far too long for him and his crown had slipped down over his eyes. "I see you're ready," he said.

Ludmilla looked down and was horrified to discover she was dressed exactly as she had been in her dream. She thought quickly. "As a matter of fact I am ready," she replied. "I've made up my mind to marry you. I have one condition though."

"And what may that be?" asked Chernomor. "You must tell me the secret of your magical powers," she replied.

Chernomor started to laugh. "You must think I'm a fool," he snorted. "If I tell you that, you'll destroy me."

"Not at all," said Ludmilla sweetly. "I just think that if we are going to be married it's important to be honest. Anyway, how could a helpless woman like me destroy such a powerful wizard?"

Chernomor's chest puffed up with pride. There was nothing he enjoyed more than being flattered. "Well, I suppose that's true," he agreed. "But what about this Ruslan fellow?"

"Oh him," said Ludmilla slyly. "He's obviously far too much of a coward to challenge you. I don't know what I saw in him."

Chernomor looked thoughtful. "Perhaps you're right," he said, "about being honest, I mean. Presumably you've noticed my rather fine beard?"

"But of course," said Ludmilla. "It's magnificent, and so very, very long."

"Ah, yes," replied Chernomor. "That's because it's never been cut. It is the source of all my magical power."

"Really?" said Ludmilla. "How interesting. So what would happen if someone cut it?"

Chernomor gave her a sharp look. "Enough of this chatter," he said. "Let's waste no more time." Grabbing her by the hand, he hurried down the stairs to the chapel.

Ludmilla's heart was pounding furiously. "What if Ruslan doesn't come?" she thought. Then a trumpet sounded.

"Wait here," ordered Chernomor, and he flew away with his beard trailing over his shoulder.

Outside, Ruslan was waiting with his sword drawn. But when the gate swung open and he saw his tiny foe he lowered it. "I'm looking for the wizard Chernomor," he said.

The dwarf swelled with indignation. "You've found him," he barked, "but you'll be sorry you did."

The next thing Ruslan knew, he was sprawling on the floor. He scrambled to his feet and thrust his sword at the dwarf, but Chernomor was too fast for him. Ruslan struck at him again and again. Even when the blows hit their target, they didn't make a scratch. He was amazed. None of his enemies had ever managed to get the better of him before, but of course none of them had had magic on their side.

When Ruslan saw Chernomor's sword come flashing through the air all by itself, he knew he was beaten. A moment later, it was pinning him to the ground. Ludmilla screamed and ran down the path towards them. "Cut off his beard!" she called.

Her cries distracted the dwarf
and his sword fell to the ground.
Ruslan made a grab for the beard,
but Chernomor was too quick.
Just as Ruslan caught hold
of it the dwarf took
to the air.

Chernomor flew over the treetops,
past the castle's highest towers and into
the clouds, with brave Ruslan still clinging
onto his beard. The wizard knew that as long as
he stayed in the air his beard was safe, for if Ruslan cut
it off he would plummet to his death.

They flew for hours, over hills and valleys, lakes and rivers,
but as the day wore on Chernomor began to tire. "Listen, why
don't we make our peace?" he suggested. "I'll put you down if..."

"I don't want to hear your ifs," Ruslan interrupted. "I don't
do deals with bride-snatchers."

Chernomor panicked. He tried everything he could to shake Ruslan off. He thrashed his head from side to side, made sudden dives and looped the loop until they both turned green. But Ruslan would not be shaken.

The dwarf-wizard was so exhausted after all this that he could barely fly. Slowly, he drifted down through the clouds and past a flock of birds.

Ruslan's feet were almost scraping the treetops when he heard someone call out his name. He looked down and saw Ludmilla running along on the ground below. They had gone around in an enormous circle and were right back where they had started. "Cut his beard off now," she shouted.

By this time, Ruslan was only a few feet away from the ground. Summoning every last bit of strength, he began to climb up the beard. The dwarf flapped his arms, trying frantically to gain some height. But it was too late. Ruslan had reached the top. He raised his sword and with a single slice he chopped off the wizard's beard.

Ruslan tumbled to the ground. Immediately, he leaped to his feet, sword at the ready.

Meanwhile, Chernomor had landed head first in a gooseberry bush. He emerged with leaves and berries sticking out of the remains of his beard. All his magic was gone. Too cowardly to face Ruslan and Ludmilla without it, he staggered away into the forest, never to be seen again.

Merlin and King Arthur

A dragon hurtled down from the sky, beating its mighty wings. King Arthur swung his sword at it, but the dragon hardly seemed to notice his blows. Seizing the king in its claws, it soared into the sky.

Only then did Arthur see what was really happening. Down below, his people were fleeing from the dragon, but the true threat lay ahead of them. Lying in wait over the hill was an army of griffins.

Arthur woke up in a cold sweat. He had only been dreaming. Even so, the images that had raged through his mind disturbed him. He went to Merlin to ask his advice.

The old wizard's beard was streaked with silver, and his wisdom was beyond this world. He listened carefully to what Arthur said and only spoke when he had finished. "Things are not always what they seem," he said solemnly. "Don't be too hasty. Learn to recognize your friends and your enemies too. Your kingdom depends on it."

Arthur sighed. Sometimes, it seemed as though Merlin was talking in riddles. Feeling frustrated, he decided to go hunting to take his mind off things.

Soon, he was riding through the forest with his friends. It wasn't long before they caught sight of a white stag. Arthur urged his horse on, taking the lead.

The stag led them
on a merry dance and after
half an hour their horses were
foaming with sweat.

When they came to a spring,
Arthur drew to a halt. "Let's stop here,"
he said. The knights drank eagerly, and
their horses did too. Then they settled
down to rest in the shade.

Arthur paced up and down by the spring.
He was still trying to make sense of his dream.
But his musings were interrupted by the sound
of hounds baying.

The noise grew louder. Then the oddest
creature Arthur had ever seen came hurtling
through the trees. It had the body of
a leopard, the head of a serpent and
the legs of a deer. The baying seemed
to be coming from its belly.

The creature stopped when it saw Arthur.
Eyeing him warily, it crouched down by the spring and
began to lap up the water. The baying grew quieter.
When it had quenched its thirst, the creature raised its
head. A forked tongue flickered from its mouth, tasting
the air. Then, suddenly, it bolted into the forest.

A few minutes later, a knight ran into the glade.
"My name is Pellinore," he panted. "Has a strange beast
passed this way?"

"Yes," said Arthur. "But you'll never
catch it on foot."

"Then give me your horse,"
demanded Pellinore. "I have
been following that beast
for a year, and I will
catch it if it's the last
thing I do."

King Arthur loved a challenge and this quest appealed to him. "You must be tired," he said. "Why don't you let me take over?"

"Never," cried Pellinore angrily. "You're a fool to suggest it. This is my destiny. If you won't give me your horse, I'll take it." Seizing the reins of Arthur's horse, he swung into the saddle and galloped away.

Arthur gazed after him, totally stunned. He felt a mixture of anger and admiration for this stranger. Determined to go after him, he borrowed a horse from one of the other knights. As he was about to set off, a boy came up to him. "You're making a mistake," he said. "This quest will distract you from your true purpose. You risk your life and your kingdom in pursuing it."

"Don't be insolent," said Arthur. "You're too young to know anything. Now step aside. I'm in a hurry."

The boy looked at him intently. "It's true that age can bring wisdom," he replied, "but the old are not always wise."

Arthur felt uncomfortable. These eyes were not those of a child. In fact, they looked strangely familiar. "Is this some sort of trick?" he asked suspiciously.

The boy shook his head. "I know about your dream," he said. "You would do well to listen to me."

"When you are old enough to carry a sword, then you can give me advice," said Arthur curtly, and set off down the path that Pellinore had taken.

Arthur soon caught up with him. "If you are worthy of my horse you may keep it, but first you must prove yourself," he said.

"Gladly," answered Pellinore. Swinging around, he charged at Arthur, who urged his horse into a gallop. Pellinore's lance struck Arthur's shield, almost jolting him out of his saddle.

They turned and charged again. This time, their lances crashed together and shattered into tiny pieces.

Both knights leaped to the ground and drew their swords. They fought like stags locking antlers, their blades clashing together again and again. Finally, their swords met with such force that Arthur's broke clean in two and the tip went flying through the air. He threw the rest of the sword down in disgust.

"Surrender or die," ordered Pellinore.

Just then, they heard a growl. They turned and saw a wolf staring at them. Its hackles were bristling, but it did not attack.

Turning back to Arthur, Pellinore raised his sword, ready to strike him dead. At once, the wolf sprang between the two knights. It was so fast that Pellinore had no time to react.

The moment the wolf's feet touched the ground, it transformed into Merlin. The wizard held up his hand. "Put down your sword," he said quietly.

"Get out of my way, old man," ordered Pellinore, though something made him lower his sword. "This is not your battle."

"Yes, it is," replied Merlin. "You don't know what you're doing. If you kill this knight, you will put this kingdom and all of us in great danger."

Pellinore frowned. "I don't understand what you mean," he said. "Who is this?"

"Don't you recognize King Arthur?" said Merlin quietly.

When Pellinore heard this, he was so afraid of Arthur's revenge that he raised his sword again.

Merlin knew he had to work swiftly. Closing his eyes, he began to murmur an enchantment. It was in a language no ordinary man could understand. Yet the power of his words was irresistible.

The spell took hold immediately and Pellinore's sword shuddered to a halt in mid-air. The veins in his neck bulged as he strained to move it, but it was as though his arm was held in an iron grip. "What have you done to me?" he groaned.

"I have stopped you from taking an action you would have lived to regret," replied Merlin.

The blood and anger drained from Pellinore's face and he collapsed on the ground. Arthur ran over. "You've killed him!" he exclaimed.

"He's just sleeping," said Merlin calmly. "Pellinore is a good knight and in time he will serve you well. You should not have angered him. I tried to warn you."

Arthur stared at Merlin. He recognized the intensity in his eyes. "That boy...it was you," he said slowly.

Merlin nodded. "You must learn to recognize wise words for their own sake, not according to who speaks them. In your eagerness for adventure, you were foolhardy. You acted quickly instead of pausing to think, and it was almost your downfall."

43

"I know," said Arthur. He looked down at his broken sword, which was lying on the ground.

Merlin read his thoughts. "Don't worry about that," he said. "You have outgrown that sword. Come with me."

Merlin took Pellinore's horse and the two of them rode through the forest until they reached a lake. "There's your new sword," said Merlin. Arthur looked where he was pointing and saw a hand reaching out of the water, clutching a sword. "It is the magic sword Excalibur," explained the wizard.

Arthur's eyes shone with longing. As he gazed across the lake towards the sword, a beautiful woman emerged from the water. "Take it," she said in a soft, melodic voice. She pointed to a boat moored nearby and then slipped back into the depths of the lake.

"That was the Lady of the Lake," said Merlin. "You should do as she says."

Together, they pulled the boat out onto the water and rowed towards the sword. When they drew close, Arthur reached out, but then he hesitated.

"Take it," whispered an echo from below.

So he did. As he pulled the sword from its scabbard, there was a blinding flash of light. An incredible sense of power surged through his body. Fighting the feeling, Arthur put the sword away.

"I think I understand you now," he said to Merlin. "There is a time to fight, but there is also a time to hold back. This is a sword fit for a true king. I will try to learn patience, and prove myself worthy of it."

The Black School

Juan waved goodbye to his parents. It would be seven years before he saw them again, but he was too distracted to think about that. He had finally arrived at the Black School, the place where young wizards came to learn the art of magic. There were dozens of other children milling around on the mountainside too.

All of a sudden, the ground began to shake. There was a loud crack and a gap opened up in the mountain. The children gathered around eagerly. This was the entrance to the Black School. It was just wide enough for one person to fit through at a time.

Juan pushed forward and climbed inside. He found himself at the top of a stone staircase that seemed to wind endlessly downwards. He followed the stairs down into the heart of the mountain, his head spinning with excitement.

At the bottom there was a cavernous hall with long, wooden tables and benches, most of which were already full. Flame torches lined the walls, casting an uncertain glow in the underground gloom. Juan found himself a space and sat down.

When all the students were seated, a sinister voice rang out. "Welcome to the Black School," it said. "I am the Dark Wizard. I will be your master during your time here."

Juan looked around to see where the voice was coming from. "The Dark Wizard never shows himself," said an older boy beside him, "although you can bet he sees everything that goes on."

Opposite them there was a red-haired boy who looked as though he had been crying. "Hello there," said Juan. "You must be new too."

"I'm Fernando," said the boy with a shy smile, which was replaced almost immediately by a look of absolute terror. Juan followed his gaze and gave a start. Reaching out of the wall behind him was a bony hand, holding a tray of food.

"You'll soon get used to it," laughed the older boy. He took the tray and began dishing out the food. Juan ate quietly, but Fernando couldn't bring himself to eat anything.

When everyone else had finished, the older boy led them down a long corridor. All along the walls there were paintings of people whose eyes seemed to follow their every move. "Here's your dormitory," he said, opening a door. "You're with the other new boys." Inside, there were lots of identical beds, with some nervous-looking boys huddled in them.

"This place is weird," whispered Fernando when the older boy had gone.

Juan nodded. "Let's get some sleep," he suggested. "I'm sure things will seem better in the morning."

Neither of them slept a wink, and they were so deep under the ground that it was impossible to tell when morning had come. Only the sound of a bell ringing told them that night was over.

Everyone washed and dressed, and hurried to their classroom for the first lesson. There were books laid out on the desks, but there was no teacher anywhere in sight.

After a few minutes, Juan opened his book. The pages were totally blank. He looked around in confusion and saw that the others were staring at their books intently. When he looked down again, the pages were no longer empty. Fiery writing was scrawling across them. "Pay attention, slowcoach," it said. "Today, you will learn how to make a shrinking potion."

The other students were already bustling around, gathering what they needed from the big jars on the shelves. "Shall we do it together?" Fernando suggested.

"Good idea," replied Juan. Soon, they were crushing dandelions, pricking themselves on nettles and chasing toads around the classroom as they tried to follow the instructions.

When they had finished, Juan found a large egg timer and turned it upside down. They heated up the potion for five minutes, until it turned bright blue. Fernando sniffed it. "Eurgh!" he said. "That smells disgusting."

"I'll go first," said Juan. He took a big swig and made a face. "It doesn't taste great either," he said.

Fernando waited for Juan to shrink. "It hasn't worked," he said in disappointment.

"Maybe it takes time," suggested Juan. "Here, you try some." Fernando grabbed the bottle and drained the rest.

By now, all the students had drunk their potions and were looking expectantly at their classmates. Then one of them gave a shout. He was getting smaller.

Within five minutes, the entire class had shrunk to the size of mice. They ran around the classroom squealing with delight.

It was quite a while before the novelty wore off. "So how do we make ourselves big again?" squeaked Fernando. They looked at one another. No one knew the answer.

"I'd better find out," said Juan. Gripping the leg of the desk tightly with his knees, he climbed slowly up. The others all held their breath until he reached the top. Juan clambered onto the desk and went over to the book. "You have learned an important lesson," he read slowly. "Always have the antidote ready before you start." Below it gave instructions for how to make it.

It wasn't easy to do things now they were all so tiny and it took most of the day to prepare the potion. When they had finally finished, Juan took a sip of it. He felt his body stretch up, like a flower reaching towards the light. Soon, all his classmates were growing too.

The rest of their lessons followed a similar pattern. They never saw a teacher; only the mysterious writing in their books told them what to do. One day, they would be hatching out dragons' eggs and the next they would be floating in mid-air. They learned how to turn one another into frogs, make themselves invisible and do all kinds of other magical things.

As the years passed by, Juan and Fernando became very accomplished young wizards. Eventually, the time came for them to graduate from the Black School. Much as they had enjoyed it, they couldn't wait to hear the birds singing and feel the warmth of the sun on their skin again.

The day before they were due to leave, Juan was busy packing up his things when Fernando rushed into the dormitory. "Have you heard?" he burst out.

"Heard what?" asked Juan.

"The Dark Wizard is going to appear at our graduation tomorrow," said Fernando. A buzz of excitement went around the dormitory. In all of their time at the Black School, none of the students had ever seen the Dark Wizard.

The next day, everyone crowded into the Great Hall, chattering excitedly.

"Silence," boomed the same sinister voice they had heard when they arrived. They looked up and saw a cloaked figure looming over them. Fernando shivered. Inside the hood, all he could see was a pair of gleaming eyes.

"Listen to me carefully," said the Dark Wizard. "Here at the Black School you have learned many things, but nothing in this life is free. One of you must pay the price for everyone. The last person left here today will never see the light of day again. You will be my slave for all eternity." He threw back his head and gave an evil laugh.

The students looked at one another fearfully, wondering whether he was serious. "Why are you still here?" roared the Dark Wizard. "Do you *all* want to stay?" The very thought of it made everyone panic and there was a mad scramble as they made a dash for the stairs.

In the rush, Fernando stumbled. Juan stopped to help him up, and they got left behind. Racing to try to catch up with the others, they bounded up the stairs two at a time.

It wasn't long before they heard the Dark Wizard coming after them. Their legs felt like lead, but they kept on going, up and up. Eventually, they came to the top. Sunlight was flooding through the crack. After so many years of darkness, the bright light was almost blinding. As they groped their way towards the opening, they heard the Dark Wizard behind them. "So..." he said, in an icy voice, "which of you will it be?"

They looked at the crack. There was only room for one person at a time. "You go," urged Juan.

"No," said Fernando. "I won't leave without you." There was a determination in his eyes that Juan hadn't seen before.

"If you can't decide which of you is to go last, I'll keep both of you," threatened the Dark Wizard.

"But we're not the last," said Fernando. "What about him?" He pointed at the wall.

The Dark Wizard looked where he was pointing and saw Fernando's shadow behind him. Mistaking it for another student, he pounced on it.

"Quickly!" hissed Fernando. He pushed Juan through the crack and tumbled out after him.

As soon as they were outside, there was a terrible grinding noise and the crack closed behind them. They could hear the wizard's angry shouts echoing around inside the mountain. The two boys looked at one another and then ran like the wind.

When they finally came to a stop, they were both panting with exhaustion. Juan bent over, holding his sides. "Look!" he exclaimed suddenly. He was pointing at the ground near Fernando's feet.

"What?" said Fernando. "I can't see anything."

"Exactly," replied Juan.

Then Fernando realized what he meant. Stretching out behind his friend was a long, dark shadow, but behind him there was nothing at all. "I suppose the Dark Wizard got to keep a little bit of me after all," laughed Fernando.

From then on, Fernando was shadowless. When people heard how he had lost his shadow, they were a little afraid. But Fernando himself was never afraid again. He had faced up to the Dark Wizard, and he had won.

An enchanted horse

Every spring, King Sabur of Persia put on an extravagant festival. People came from far and wide to join in the frivolities, and many of them brought gifts for the king. This year, one gift stood out from all the rest.

When an old man shuffled into the court dressed in shabby clothes, the king wasn't expecting much. "My gift is outside," announced the man with a bow, although he was already so bent over that his bow was barely noticeable.

The king and his courtiers followed him into the garden, where they found a life-sized ebony horse. It was exquisitely crafted. Its body was adorned with intricate patterns, the stirrups were made of solid gold and the saddle was decorated with sparkling jewels. "It's beautiful," murmured the king admiringly.

"It's much more than that," replied the old man. "Watch this." He clambered into the saddle and turned a tiny brass key on the horse's neck. There was a gentle whirring noise and to everyone's amazement the horse launched into the air.

The king's mouth gaped open as the horse flew over the treetops. Higher and higher it went, until it looked no bigger than a fly. It circled three times and then began to descend.

When the horse landed in the courtyard, the king hurried over. "How did you do that?" he asked the old man excitedly.

The sorcerer (for what else could he be?) gave a twisted smile. "It's magic," he whispered.

"What a truly wonderful gift!" exclaimed the king. "I've never seen anything like it. Please name your reward. Whatever you desire will be yours."

"There's just one thing I would like," replied the old man, "and that's your daughter's hand in marriage."

The king hesitated, but he was a man of his word and so he had no choice but to agree.

When the princess found out, she was devastated. "How could my own father do this to me?" she wailed. "That man must be at least a hundred years old."

Her desperate cries soon reached the ears of her brother, Prince Kamar, who came to see what was wrong. "If you'd seen the person I must marry, you wouldn't need to ask," the princess sobbed. "I'm sure Father has been bewitched by this horse."

The prince marched straight to see the king. "Have you lost your mind?" he stormed. "Would you marry off your daughter against her will for the sake of a mere toy?"

"Ah, but you haven't seen it yet," countered the king, his enthusiasm undampened. "Come and have a look." The prince examined the horse and he had to admit that it was very impressive. "Climb on," urged his father. "Wait until you see it fly."

Prince Kamar didn't need much encouragement. He swung himself into the saddle and flicked the reins.

Nothing happened. "I thought this was supposed to be a flying horse," he scoffed.

This was too much for the sorcerer, who had been listening to the prince's insolence with growing impatience. "Allow me," he said, turning the key. At once, the horse lurched into the air.

Taken by surprise, the prince fell forward onto the horse's neck. He clutched at its mane as the ground slipped away beneath him. After just a few moments, he was already so high that the people looked like ants scurrying around below and the trees seemed no bigger than flowers in a garden. From even higher up, he could see rivers winding like silver snakes through the mountains and down to the sea.

The prince shivered as the horse flew up through the clouds. "This is high enough," he thought. Then his heart sank, for he realized the sorcerer hadn't told him how to get down. He tried turning the key the other way, but the horse kept on rising. "The old man is trying to kill me," gasped the prince.

Meanwhile, down on the ground, the same thought was dawning on the king. "What have you done?" he said to the sorcerer. "Bring back my son immediately."

"I'm afraid that's impossible," replied the old man. "I can't control the horse from down here and unfortunately your son didn't wait to hear all the instructions. There's nothing I can do."

The king was furious. "Throw him into the dungeon," he ordered his guards.

Of course, this didn't help his son, who was beginning to think he might never get down. The prince tried to concentrate. "What goes up must come down," he reasoned, and began to search for another key. Eventually, he found one, hidden inside the horse's ear. It was so small that it was difficult to grip, but he managed to turn it.

The horse paused for a moment and then began to descend. Prince Kamar fiddled with the keys, turning them this way and that. He managed to work out how to control the horse and soon he could steer it whichever way he wanted.

It was starting to get dark, so when the prince saw a palace a little way below he guided the horse towards it. Down, down, down it flew, and landed with perfect precision on the rooftop.

Prince Kamar wasn't sure whether he would be welcome there, so he waited until it was completely dark before creeping into the palace to explore.

As he tiptoed along the corridors, he noticed a light coming from one of the rooms. He went closer and found the door ajar. Inside, a beautiful young woman was lying asleep.

The prince crept over and knelt down beside her. The girl's eyes fluttered open. When she saw him, she opened her mouth to cry out, but he touched his finger to her soft lips and begged her not to give him away. "Who are you?" she whispered.

"I am your humble servant," he said. "A happy adventure has brought me here from a faraway land." He told her his story and she listened, enraptured, to every word. The prince was so charming and handsome that she found herself falling in love with him.

The next morning, one of the maids popped her head around the door to wake the princess. When she found a stranger in the room, she screamed for help. Immediately, soldiers came rushing from every corner of the palace.

The princess's father burst in, his sword drawn. "Villain!" he shouted. "Get away from my daughter."

"I am not a villain," said the prince calmly. "I am Prince Kamar of Persia, and I would like to marry the princess."

His words took the wind out of the king's sails, leaving him lost for words. "Allow me to prove myself," said the prince. "Send your whole army against me. If they defeat me, then all is lost. But if they don't, you must allow me to marry your daughter."

"Very well," agreed the king. "I will have a horse ready for you at midday."

"That won't be necessary," Prince Kamar replied. "I have my own horse up on the roof."

"On the roof!" repeated the king. "Have you lost your mind? It's impossible to get a horse up there."

"Well, that's where it is," said the prince patiently.

The bewildered king sent his soldiers to investigate, and sure enough they found the ebony horse on the roof. They brought it down, staggering under the weight.

The king started to laugh when he saw the horse.
"It's nothing more than a wooden toy," he said.

The soldiers carried it out to the battlefield, giggling among themselves. Prince Kamar took no notice. He watched the army line up against him, and then climbed onto the horse. "I'm ready," he declared.

The king gave the signal and there was a thunder of hooves as the army charged. Prince Kamar reached down and turned the brass key. With one enormous leap, the ebony horse bounded right over the soldiers' heads.

The army was thrown into chaos. The horses at the front stopped abruptly, catapulting the soldiers over their heads, while the horses behind crowded into the riderless steeds. "Stop him," bellowed the king. "He's escaping." But Prince Kamar was already out of reach.

"Take me with you," called the princess from the roof of the palace. The prince circled and landed beside her.

The princess was not afraid. She climbed onto the horse and wrapped her arms around Prince Kamar's waist. Then away they flew. She held on tightly as they soared over mountains and valleys, forests and deserts.

Finally, they landed at King Sabur's summer palace, just a short distance from Prince Kamar's home. "Wait here," said the prince. "I'll go ahead and tell my father you're coming. Then I'll come for you when everything's ready." Leaving the ebony horse with her, he continued on foot.

When Prince Kamar's father saw him, he was overwhelmed with emotion. "I thought that cursed sorcerer had killed you," he wept. "I've had him thrown into the dungeon."

"I'm sure he didn't mean any harm," said Prince Kamar generously. "Anyway, all that's in the past now." Then he told his father everything that had happened.

The king was so happy that he not only agreed to release the sorcerer, he piled precious jewels upon him too. But he made no mention of the marriage to his daughter.

The sorcerer's heart was black with bitterness. As he slunk from the court, he silently vowed to take his revenge.

An opportunity presented itself sooner than he expected. On his way out, he overheard two of the guards talking about Prince Kamar and the princess, and discovered that the prince had left her waiting at the king's summer palace.

The sorcerer hurried there at once and found his very own magic horse standing by the pavilion. He hobbled over to it, delighted to be reunited with his treasure.

When the princess saw him, she assumed he must be one of the king's servants. "Have you come for me?" she asked eagerly, although when he turned to face her the look of anger in his eyes made her take a step back.

The sorcerer nodded. "Prince Kamar sent me," he said. "We'll ride on the ebony horse."

At this, the princess smiled, for she thought that anyone who could ride the horse must have been sent by the prince.

The old man climbed on and helped her up in front of him. Then he turned the key and away they flew, in the opposite direction from the one Prince Kamar had taken. "Where are you going?" asked the princess in alarm.

"They made me a promise," the sorcerer growled, "and if they won't give me what's mine I will take what's theirs."

"I don't *belong* to anyone," said the princess defiantly, "and I'm certainly not going anywhere with you." She had seen the prince control the horse and knew what to do. Reaching into the horse's ear she turned the hidden key. Immediately, the horse did a nose-dive.

The sorcerer lunged for the other key, but the princess was too fast for him. She grabbed both keys and threw them away. "What have you done?" he screeched, looking for a moment as though he was going to dive after them.

"I've put an end to this nonsense," retorted the princess bravely, although by now she was rather concerned at how quickly the ground was approaching.

The horse hurtled down
towards King Sabur's orchard,
picking up more and more speed.
The princess screamed as it crashed
through the treetops. Luckily, her clothes
caught on the branches, breaking her fall.
But the ebony horse dropped like a stone
and smashed to smithereens on the ground.

The princess found herself dangling from a branch.
She was dazed, but unharmed.

"My precious horse," howled the sorcerer, who was
hanging a little way below. He jumped down and
staggered towards what was left of his creation.

The palace guards were waiting for him.
"Arrest that man," commanded King Sabur.

Prince Kamar helped the princess down.
Although he was delighted to see her,
he was sad about the horse. "It was
beautiful," she said, "but it's been
nothing but trouble."

"That's not quite
true," he answered.
"It helped me to
find you, and for
that I'll always
be grateful."

The miserable king

Giuseppe took off his spectacles and rubbed his eyes. It was late and he was still huddled over his books. "Is everything all right?" asked an anxious voice behind him.

Giuseppe looked up distractedly. "Erm...yes," he mumbled. "I've just got to finish this job for the king." His granddaughter, Elfie, stepped forward. She had brought him a mug of cocoa, as she did every night. Giuseppe smiled, but although his smile was warm his eyes looked tired.

Elfie walked away sadly. When she reached the door, she looked back. "Grandpa, can't I help?" she asked.

"Certainly not," said her grandfather, his voice unusually sharp. "Magic can be very dangerous. It's not for little girls to play around with."

Tears welled up in Elfie's eyes. Before Giuseppe could see them, she ran to her room.

Elfie was desperately worried. Since the queen died, the king had become more and more difficult. It was her grandfather, the court wizard, who suffered most, as the king set him increasingly ridiculous tasks.

67

This time the king had asked him to conjure up a floating palace of gold in the queen's memory. As Elfie stared out of the window, she gave a sigh. Surely it was impossible. But just then a stream of shimmering lights swirled down from the sky. "Fairies," she gasped.

Down below, Elfie's grandfather was waving his wand wildly. The fairies danced through the air, following its every move. Behind them, they left a trail of golden dust. When morning came, the sun shone through the dust, revealing a beautiful floating palace.

With their work complete, the fairies fluttered away, like butterflies on a summer breeze. Elfie's heart swelled with pride as she gazed at the palace. Incredibly, her grandfather had done it again.

When the king flung open his curtains, even he was impressed. He thought he had asked the impossible, but there it was: a golden palace fit for a queen floating in the air before him. He rang the bell beside his bed.

Giuseppe straightened his robes and hurried to see the king. "At your service," he said with a bow. "I hope the palace I have made pleases you."

"I suppose it's attractive enough," said the king, "but it won't bring back my queen."

"Of course not, Your Majesty," agreed Giuseppe. "Nothing could do that."

The king glared at him. "Then what use is it?" he barked. "And what use are you?"

The wizard said nothing. Grief had made the king unpredictable and he was worried about provoking him. But his silence didn't help the king's dark mood.

"It's been so long since I laughed, I've almost forgotten how," said the king mournfully. "If you're so clever, you must make me laugh again. I'll give you until this time tomorrow, and if you can't do it you'll lose your head."

"I'll do my very best," promised Giuseppe, although secretly he couldn't help feeling worried.

69

Swan Lake

It was the day before Prince Siegfried's twenty-first birthday, but he was far from happy about it. Tomorrow his mother was holding a grand ball and there he would have to choose his bride. "It's not fair. I'm much too young to get married," he grumbled to one of his friends.

"Don't worry about it," his friend replied. "Anything could happen before tomorrow. A few of us are going hunting now. Why don't you come with us?"

Siegfried adored hunting. "Great idea," he said with a grin. "Give me two minutes."

Soon, the friends were galloping through the forest on their horses, with the wind rushing through their hair. Siegfried was in his element. He galloped faster and faster, leaving the others far behind.

After a while, he came to a lake. It was a deep, mournful blue and Siegfried felt strangely drawn to it. He reined in his horse and got down to take a look.

Gliding across the water was a group of swans. In the soft light of dusk they looked almost ghostly. As they swam closer, Siegfried noticed that one of them was wearing a small crown.

It paused in front of him and bowed its head demurely. Then its eyes lifted to meet his. "I have never seen such beauty," the prince murmured.

No sooner had the words left
Siegfried's lips than the swan turned into
a beautiful young maiden. She had long, golden hair and was
dressed all in white. "Who are you?" whispered Siegfried, hardly
daring to breathe in case this vision of loveliness fled.

"My name is Odette," she said. "I am under an enchantment.
The sorcerer von Rothbart has turned me into a swan. Only at
night may I return to my true form."

"But why would he do such a cruel thing?" asked Siegfried.

"He was jealous because everyone thought I was more
beautiful than his daughter," explained Odette sorrowfully.

A tear trickled down her face and splashed into the water. "This lake is full of tears," she said. "After von Rothbart cast the spell on me, my parents came here every day to visit. They wept until they could weep no more, but it was no use."

Siegfried's heart filled with pity. He took her hand and helped her out of the water. "Can nothing be done?" he asked.

"It's not so easy," she said. "Only true love can set me free. If I can find someone who will always be faithful, then the spell will be broken."

At that moment, an owl flew down and landed in a nearby tree. Siegfried and Odette were so absorbed in one another that neither of them saw it, but it was watching them very carefully indeed.

"I've got an idea," said Siegfried eagerly. "Will you come to a ball at the palace tomorrow?"

Odette smiled at Siegfried. "I'll gladly come," she said. Overcome with happiness, Siegfried swept her up in his arms. Slowly, they began to dance. There was no music except for the beating of their hearts, but they were perfectly in time with one another. It was as though they had always been together.

The other swans drifted in and out of the reeds, their long necks swaying gracefully as they tried to get a better look.

It hardly seemed a moment before the first glow of morning appeared. "I must go now," said the swan maiden, "but I will come tonight. Wait for me." She turned to go and, in a flurry of feathers, became a swan once more.

Siegfried could hardly bear to tear himself away, but he had to get home for the ball. Springing onto his horse, he galloped away through the forest.

He wasn't the only one who was in a hurry. As soon as Siegfried was out of sight, the owl sped silently away. It kept on flying until it came to a ruined castle deep in the forest. A pale face was peering out of one of the windows, impatiently watching and waiting.

The owl swept in through the window and turned into none other than von Rothbart himself. His daughter, Odile, was standing there with her arms folded. "Where have you been?" she whined.

"Looking for a husband for you," replied von Rothbart. "And, as it happens, I seem to have found one."

"Who is it?" she asked suspiciously. No one had ever shown the slightest interest in her. If her black looks and foul temper weren't enough to put suitors off, then the fact that her father was a sorcerer certainly was.

"Never mind. Just do as I tell you," snapped von Rothbart. Questions always made him irritable.

Back at the palace, preparations for the ball were well underway when Siegfried rode up. "Look at the state of you," scolded his mother. "I'm not even going to ask where you've been. Just make sure you're ready before the guests arrive."

Siegfried gave a sigh and went up to his room. He lay down on his bed and stared up at the ceiling, thinking about Odette. He couldn't get her out of his mind. Only when it grew dark outside did he finally begin to get ready. Dressed in his finest clothes, he went downstairs to wait for the guests.

His friends were already there. "Here comes the reluctant groom," teased one as he approached.

"Very funny," muttered Siegfried.

"So what happened to you yesterday?" asked another. "We looked everywhere for you."

"Oh, I got lost," Siegfried replied casually.

His friends didn't think anything of it and began to chatter about hunting. For once, Siegfried didn't join in. There was a faraway look in his eyes. He didn't even object when his mother came over to smooth down his hair.

It was the sound of a trumpet fanfare that brought him back down to earth. The first guests were arriving. Siegfried looked eagerly over to the door, but Odette wasn't among them. He turned away in disappointment.

His mother took him by the arm. "Come along," she said. "Don't be shy." Then, with great ceremony, she began to introduce him to his potential brides.

The first had a voice so shrill it made his ears hurt, the second fidgeted as if she had ants in her petticoat and the third had teeth so big he thought she might eat him alive.

Siegfried turned to his mother and shrugged helplessly, but she was already busy lining up more eligible ladies. They trod on his feet when they danced with him, squeezing him until he could hardly breathe. Even those that weren't totally hideous just didn't compare with his swan maiden.

By now, Siegfried was starting to worry. It was getting late and there was still no sign of Odette. Then a murmur went around the room.

He turned and saw an elegant young woman dressed all in black coming into the hall with a male companion. Her face was covered with a veil.

Siegfried went over to pay his respects, and was surprised to find that her companion was von Rothbart the sorcerer. He hadn't been invited, but Siegfried didn't feel he could turn a guest away. Instead, he bowed to him politely and then turned to the lady. "I don't believe we've met," he said, kissing her hand.

She lifted her veil. "It's you!" exclaimed Siegfried, for gazing back at him was Odette's beautiful face. He waited until von Rothbart was busy talking and took her aside. "What are you doing with *him*?" whispered Siegfried.

"It was the only way I could come," she replied.

Siegfried looked at her intently. There was something not quite right about her...a hint of darkness in her eyes. "You seem different," he said.

"Do I?" she said stiffly. "I'm sorry. I suppose I'm just tired."

Her voice was so cold it made Siegfried shiver. She didn't seem at all like his gentle Odette, but she looked exactly like her. Unable to resist her beauty, he asked her to dance.

They whirled around the hall, with her mirroring his every step like a shadow.

All the other guests stopped to watch. They nudged one another and pushed forward to get a clearer view. The two of them looked for all the world like the perfect couple.

Deep in his heart Siegfried knew that there was nothing between them. Yet, when everyone began to clap and cheer, he pushed his doubts to the back of his mind.

He didn't see the real Odette's pale, sad face appear at the window. He didn't hear the pounding of her heart when she saw him dancing with another woman. And he could never have imagined the pain she felt as she watched him take out a ring and ask Odile to marry him.

Odette had seen enough. She turned to run away, but she stumbled and knocked over a flowerpot. Everyone in the hall looked over at the window to see what the noise was. "I will," answered Odile quickly. It was loud enough for them all to hear.

As Odette scrambled to her feet, her eyes caught Siegfried's. The briefest of looks said everything. Desperate to escape, she turned and fled. As she ran, her arms turned into snow-white wings. Half-running, half-flying, she disappeared into the forest.

Inside the hall, a horrible laugh rang out. "It seems that love really is blind," mocked von Rothbart. "You have proposed to my daughter in front of all these people, and now you must marry her."

Siegfried turned to Odile in confusion. Her eyes narrowed and her mouth curled into a sneer. The spell was broken. This was not his lovely swan maiden. It was the sorcerer's vile daughter.

"What have I done?" whispered Siegfried. He staggered from the palace and ran towards the stables. He had to find his beloved Odette.

Moments later, he was galloping through the forest. He rode faster than he had ever ridden before and in no time at all he reached the lake. Odette was lying beside it with her wings covering her head, sobbing as though her heart would break.

Siegfried went over and knelt down beside her. "I'm so sorry," he said softly.

She looked up. "It's not your fault," she said. "But now the spell can never be broken. I must live as a swan forever."

"Then I will stay with you," said Siegfried. "I love you and I'll do whatever it takes to be with you." He kissed her gently on the lips. As he did, his chest swelled and suddenly he felt strong and free.

Siegfried looked down. White feathers were sprouting all along his arms. He was turning into a swan. He looked at Odette and saw that her body was changing too. "Is this the only way we can be together?" he asked.

She nodded anxiously.

"Then let's fly away," he said.

Odette's face brightened. Together, they ran out onto the lake, wings outstretched. Their feet skimmed over the surface of the water until they picked up enough speed to soar into the air.

They kept on flying until they were far, far away from the sorcerer and his daughter.

They found their new life strange at first, but this only made them closer. They became the most faithful of companions and lived happily together for the rest of their lives.

The tree wizards

Once there was a young goatherd named Finn who lived in the hills with his goats. Day after day, he would drift along without a care in the world, playing his pipes and daydreaming. Then, one day, as he wandered down to the river, he saw a girl sitting beside the water making a flower garland. She was very pretty, with jet-black hair and pale white skin.

Finn sat down a little way away and began to play his pipes softly. "What's that dreadful noise?" said the girl in a sharp voice. Finn looked up. She was staring at him, a deep frown creasing her pretty forehead.

He smiled apologetically. "Sorry, I didn't mean to disturb you," he said.

"It's a bit late for that," snapped the girl, and she picked up her garland and marched off.

Finn gazed after her longingly. In spite of her rudeness, he had fallen in love. For the next few weeks, he could think of nothing else. "I must go and find her," he decided at last.

Abandoning his goats, Finn went down into the valley. He tramped from village to village and eventually he found an old man who recognized the description. "Ah yes, that will be Naina," he said knowingly. "I'd be careful of that one if I were you."

But Finn was very insistent, so the man told him where she lived. When Finn arrived at Naina's house, he stopped outside and took a deep breath. Then he knocked at the door.

"Who is it?" came a voice from inside.

"It's Finn, the goatherd," said Finn.

Naina threw open the door. "What do you want?" she said.

"I j-j-just wanted to see you," stammered Finn. "I think I'm in love with you."

She tossed her head. "Well, that doesn't surprise me at all," she replied haughtily. "But what's it to me? You're nothing but a smelly goatherd."

Finn's heart sank. She was right — he had nothing to offer a girl like her. He didn't even have a herd of goats any more. "I must find a way to prove myself," he thought.

He decided to try his luck on the high seas, and set sail on a merchant's ship the very next day. For ten years, the sea was Finn's home. He fought in battles with treasure-hungry pirates and found adventure in far-flung lands, but not a day went by when he didn't think of Naina.

When he returned, a rich man, the first thing he did was look for his beloved. He found her at the marketplace with her friends. She was more beautiful than ever, but her heart was still as cold as ice. "Do I know you?" she said when he tapped her on the shoulder.

"We met by the river a long time ago," said Finn. "I came to see you at your house."

Naina stared at him. He was dressed in an elegant coat and wore shiny shoes with silver buckles on them. "Not the goatherd?" she said in surprise.

"Yes!" exclaimed Finn, delighted that she remembered him. "Well, not any more," he added quickly. "Things have changed."

Naina's friends nudged one another excitedly. It wasn't every day that such a fine young man turned up out of the blue.

"I've brought you a gift," said Finn, and held out a wooden chest.

When he opened the chest, Naina's friends' eyes almost popped out of their heads. It was full of all kinds of dazzling jewels. Naina just turned up her pretty nose. "You can't *buy* love," she said, although she took the chest all the same.

Feeling foolish, Finn hung his head and walked away. He returned to the hills, but life there was lonely now. One day, he sat down beside the river and began to weep. "I can't live without her," he sobbed.

"Perhaps I can help," said a voice. An old man was standing over him.

"Who are you?" asked Finn.

"I belong to a guild of wizards who live in the forest," explained the old man. "We've been watching you for some time. You're an interesting case. For hundreds of years we have been trying to discover love's secrets. We'd like to help you, if we may."

"Please do," said Finn. "I'll do whatever it takes to make her love me."

"Very well," said the wizard. "Come with me." He led Finn deep into the heart of the forest, where only a little sunlight filtered through the dense trees. "Here we are," announced the wizard.

Finn looked around, puzzled. He
could see nothing but trees. Then one of
them stepped forward and he almost jumped
out of his skin. It stretched out a branch as if
to greet him.

Hesitantly, Finn took hold of the branch
and shook it. As he did so, the tree bark melted
away and Finn found himself face to face with
another wizard. "Welcome," the wizard said.
"We've been waiting for you."

Finn watched in disbelief as, one by one,
the trees around him turned into wizards too.
There were twelve of them altogether, each
wearing a long, green robe that blended in
perfectly with the forest.

"Let's waste no more time," said the first wizard, who seemed to be in charge. The other wizards set to work at once, searching through their spell books for ideas.

After a few days, they came up with a plan. It was simple, but terribly romantic. They taught Finn a spell and he set off for Naina's house.

"Come outside, my love," he called to her. "I have something for you."

When she opened the door, he whispered the magic words and fragrant petals swirled down from the sky. "They are not nearly as sweet as you," said Finn, "but I hope they please you."

Naina gave an enormous sneeze. "They certainly don't," she said. "I don't love you and it will take more than a silly trick like that to change my mind."

Slowly and sadly, Finn made his way back to the forest. The wizards were waiting eagerly, but Finn's long face told them all they needed to know. "Don't worry," the chief wizard reassured him. "We haven't finished yet."

The wizards whispered together for a long time. Then they dragged a cauldron out of the bushes and began mixing together all kinds of strange plants. Finn helped in whatever way he could, crushing flowers and chopping up herbs. When they had finished, the chief wizard took the tail feather of a nightingale and dipped it into the mixture by the light of the full moon.

The next morning, Finn took the feather and hurried to Naina's house. "Lovely Naina, come and see what I have brought for you," he called.

When she opened the door, he held out the feather. "It's for you," he announced proudly.

"Yuck!" said Naina. "What would I want with a grubby old feather?"

"Ah, but this is no ordinary feather," said Finn. He blew on it softly and the songs of a thousand nightingales filled the air in the most beautiful serenade imaginable.

Naina covered her ears with her hands. "What a racket! Can't you just leave me alone?" she screeched, and ran inside.

"Never mind," said the chief wizard when Finn returned. "We'll come up with another idea. Just you wait and see."

All day, every day, the wizards sat around, searching the unfathomable depths of their minds for an answer to Finn's problem. Then, at night, they gazed up at the stars and drew strange diagrams in their notebooks. Finn waited patiently, tiptoeing around so as not to disturb them.

It was a whole year before they finally came up with another plan. "This is sure to charm her," said the chief wizard, and he told Finn what to do.

This time, Finn waited until nightfall before he went to see Naina. He knocked quietly at her door.

It was some time before she answered and when she did she wasn't happy. "What time do you call this?" she grumbled.

Finn didn't say a word. He just reached up into the sky and took down a star. Tenderly, he tucked it into her hair. "My darling Naina," he whispered, "won't you love me?"

Naina was quietly impressed, but it was not enough to make her love him. "Don't you know the meaning of the word 'no'?" she said in exasperation.

Feeling totally despondent, Finn stumbled back to the forest to find the wizards. "It's no use," he told them. "She's never going to fall in love with me."

The wizards were starting to have their doubts too. Yet they were determined to keep on trying.

As the years went by, the wizards' beards grew longer and longer, although they never seemed to get any older. They devoted their lives to solving the mystery of love.

The more time Finn spent with them, the wiser he became, and in the end it was he who found the answer, deep in his own heart. "These clever tricks will never convince her," he said. "We just need to make her feel what I feel. A simple transfer spell would do it."

"Of course," cried the chief wizard. "We should have thought of it before."

Finn muttered the spell all the way to Naina's house so that he wouldn't forget it. When he arrived, he stood outside and chanted, "Cruel girl, put yourself in my shoes. Throw open your heart; you have nothing to lose."

As the door opened, Finn's face fell. This was not the girl he remembered. Although he'd never realized it, time had stood still in the forest and he hadn't aged a bit, but in the world outside it had raced on as usual.

The years had not been kind to Naina. Endless frowns had left deep furrows in her brow, and her mouth was twisted into a snarl. Yet her eyes sparkled with something that Finn knew only too well: the light of love. It was just what he had longed for. Not any more, though. "I can't stay," he muttered.

Naina grabbed his hand. "Come here, my love," she cackled. "I think it's about time we were married." Filled with horror, he snatched it away and fled. "I love you," called Naina, hobbling after him. But this only made Finn run faster.

When he was a good distance from the village, Finn stopped to rest. Before long he heard Naina catching up. He groaned and hurried on, dodging through the forest until he found the wizards. "Quick, hide me," he panted.

The wizards were completely bemused, but they did as he asked and made him invisible.

A few moments later, when Naina stumbled into view, they understood why. "Have you seen a handsome young goatherd?" she rasped.

The wizards all shook their heads solemnly, and she continued on her way. Only when they were sure she had gone did they make Finn visible again. "So it worked," said the chief wizard.

"Oh, it worked all right," said Finn, "and it's cured my love sickness for good."

The wizard chuckled. "This love business is a strange thing," he observed. "I'm not sure I'll ever understand it."

First published in 2007 by Usborne Publishing Ltd,
Usborne House, 83-85 Saffron Hill, London EC1N 8RT, England.
www.usborne.com Copyright © 2007 Usborne Publishing Ltd.
The name Usborne and the devices ♀ 🎈 are Trade Marks of Usborne Publishing Ltd.
First published in America in 2008. U.E. Printed in Dubai.